Tiger
AND THE
Temper Tantrum

For Ruby

KINGFISHER
Larousse Kingfisher Chambers Inc.
95 Madison Avenue
New York, New York 10016

First published in 1999
2 4 6 8 10 9 7 5 3 1
1(1TR)/1298/SC/PW/NYM150

Text copyright © Vivian French 1999
Illustrations copyright © Rebecca Elgar 1999

LIBRARY OF CONGRESS CATALOGING-IN-PUBLICATION DATA
French, Vivian.
Tiger and the temper tantrum / by Vivian French;
illustrated by Rebecca Elgar—1st ed.
p. cm.
Summary: Tiger says "No!" to everything his mother wants him to
do, but then finds out that having a temper tantrum will not get him
what he wants.
[1. Temper tantrums—Fiction. 2. Behavior—Fiction. 3. Tigers—
Fiction.] I. Elgar, Rebecca, ill. II. Title.
PZ7.F88917Tig 1999 [E]—dc21 98-48756 CIP AC

ISBN 0-7534-5197-2

Printed in Hong Kong/China

Tiger
AND THE
Temper Tantrum

Vivian French & Rebecca Elgar

99
KINGFISHER
NEW YORK

"Eat up, Tiger,"
said Mother Tiger.

"No," said Tiger.
"I don't like eggs.
I want to go to the park
and climb to the top
of the jungle gym."

"We'll go to the park after
we go to the store," said
Mother Tiger.

store

"Hurry up, Tiger," said Mother Tiger. She wrapped him in his scarf. "Do you want to ride in your stroller?"

"No," said Tiger. "I want to walk. I want to walk to the park and climb to the top of the jungle gym."

In the store Tiger picked up a big bag of candy.

"Put that back, Tiger," said Mother Tiger.

"NO!" said Tiger. "I want candy to eat when I go to the park and climb to the top of the jungle gym!"

Mother Tiger put the candy back.

Outside the store Tiger threw his scarf on the ground.

"Tiger," said Mother Tiger, "pick up your scarf."

"No!" Tiger growled. "I won't! I want to go to the park! I want to climb to the top of the jungle gym— and I want to go NOW!!!" And he rolled on the ground, waving his paws.

Mother Tiger looked at Tiger.

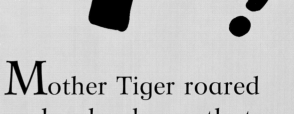

Mother Tiger roared such a loud roar that Tiger jumped.

"NO," said Mother Tiger. "We're NOT going to the park. We're going HOME. And we're going home RIGHT NOW!"

Tiger stared.

aaaah!

Tiger burst into tears.
Mother Tiger scooped him
up and into his stroller.
Tiger cried louder.
Mother Tiger walked faster.

"Hi, Tiger!" said a voice.

Tiger stopped crying.

"I'm going to the park," said Crocodile.

Tiger sniffed loudly.

"Hi, Tiger!" said Hippo as he skipped by. "I'm going to the park!"

"WAAAAAAH!!!! It's not fair!" Tiger wailed. "Everybody's going to the park except me!"

Mother Tiger stopped.

"Tiger," she said, "maybe Crocodile and Hippo don't throw temper tantrums. Maybe Crocodile and Hippo are good little animals . . . and good little animals get to go to the park!"

Tiger thought very hard.

"Do good little tigers get to go?" he asked.

"YES!" said Mother Tiger. "Going to the park with good little tigers is FUN!"

"Oh," said Tiger, and he wiped his eyes with his tail. He smoothed his fur with his claws. He smiled a HUGE smile.

"I'm a good tiger now," he said. "A VERY GOOD TIGER!"

And he was—
all the way to the top
of the jungle gym.